Anonymous

The Centennial Frog

And other Stories

Anonymous

The Centennial Frog
And other Stories

ISBN/EAN: 9783744750363

Printed in Europe, USA, Canada, Australia, Japan

Cover: Foto ©Andreas Hilbeck / pixelio.de

More available books at **www.hansebooks.com**

THE

CENTENNIAL FROG,

AND OTHER STORIES.

PHILADELPHIA:

CLAXTON, REMSEN & HAFFELFINGER,

624, 626 & 628 MARKET STREET.

1877.

Selheimer & Moore, Printers,
501 Chestnut Street.

Dedicated to

YOUNG "BIRD DEFENDERS."

CONTENTS

vii

O N the great "Centennial
Fourth,"
By unanimous Frogmarsh
vote,
Young Lieutenant Crocio
Frog
Was selected to devote
His great talents in a cause
Dear to every Frogmarsh
breast.
'T was in vain that the Lieu-
tenant
Did quite modestly pro-
test.

Best buff jerkin then he
donned,
Tuned his croak to pleas-
ant pitch;

9

From what rostrum then debated
   Should he best a throng bewitch.
Whilst on this he meditated,
   Under the lee of a big stone,

His old mother, hoarse and shaky,
   Begged not to be left alone.
"Dear old Granny," thus he soothed her,
   " In a trice I will return ;
But this day I must deliver
   Thoughts which in my bosom burn."

Gravely then Lieutenant Frog
  Leaped across their shining brook,
Through lush meadows to a garden,
  Where he stopped to take a look.
Many children here were gathered —
  Frances, Mary, Elsie, Grey,
Agnes, Anna, Arthur, Marie,
  Herbert, orator of the day.
Remnants of a feast were scattered,
  Largess to the garden-plot;
Our Lieutenant thought the sunshine
  Never brightened sweeter spot.

Smile and dimple circled freely,
  When the orator arose;
One small fleck of golden sunlight
  Danced upon his classic (?) nose.
"Friends! Companions! I this — hem — day!
  This — hem — great — hem — Centennial day!
Hem — a frog is in my throat,
  And impedes what I would say."

Lieutenant Frog, warmed and excited,—
  Hard of hearing in one ear,—

Here leaped up on Herbert's shoulder,
  That the better he might hear.

Peal on peal of wildest laughter,
  Sudden somersaults and cries;
Clapping, stamping, loud huzzas,
  Followed by exhausted sighs,
Greeted this sure confirmation
  Of the presence of a Frog;
Whilst Lieutenant stared around him,
  Solemn as a pedagogue,
Grateful for his warm reception,
  Pleased with such loud, long applause,
Waited with polite attention
  For the orator's next clause.

When the clamor had subsided,
  Grey then civilly suggested
That the far-famed eloquence
  Of Lieutenant Frog be tested.
Motion warmly seconded
  By the whole assembled throng,
With amendment that the speech
  Be forerunner of a song.

" Grey then civilly suggested
That the far-famed eloquence
Of Lieutenant Frog be tested."

Lieutenant Frog, quite charmed and flattered
   By such ready recognition
Of the rare and varied talent
   Found in Frog of his position,
Graciously did signify,
   By a most melodious croak,
He was willing to accede,
   And the following words he spoke:

"My Frog heart leaps high within me!
   Warmed with hopes of pleasing shape!
Not mere fancies made of moonshine,
   But material form they take.
Yesternight, sweet trembling rumors
   Floated in among the rushes,
Reeds, and lilies of our brook.
   In the soft, warm evening hushes
We forgot our even-croak,
   Listening to the murmured story
Of a youthful, humane band
   Covering themselves with glory!
Swelling list of 'Bird Defenders!'
   Honored champions! to-day,

The sweetest tribute to your praise
  Is from sweet Birds in roundelay!"

Lieutenant Frog's rich frogly voice
  Husky grew with his great theme;
North-west corner of his eye
  With a tear did brightly beam.
Then he grew quite bland, and smiled
  Down upon the little throng;
And resumed from Herbert's shoulder,
  In a voice now weak, now strong —
(For Lieutenant, quite unused
  To this style of declamation,
Did experience, through his frame,
  Quite a new and queer sensation,)
"As the changing seasons roll
  O'er this brave and prosperous Land,
Will there rise another army
  Who for *Frogs* will take a stand?"!!

(Here Lieutenant rolled his orbs
  In a fierce and martial style;
And I fear his primrose jerkin
  Was strained sorely for awhile.)

Quite unanimous the cheering,
   When Lieutenant's speech did close;
And he felt so very weary
   That he was inclined to dose.
But the civil Arthur hinted,
   By a sudden clever jerk,
That, "as Crocio a song had promised,
   'T was no time for him to shirk."

Lieutenant Frog, with weary smile,
   Half felt what Arthur did,
And quite the half of what he heard
   From his fine memory slid.
The warmth of that sweet afternoon
   Lulled him to calm repose;
He slept the sleep of all the just,
   One inch from Herbert's nose.

"Now this will never do," Grey cried;
   "The 'Fourth' begins to wane,
And in those clouds there surely are
   Huge bucketfuls of rain."
Thus urged by unforeseen events
   Their song then to demand,

They tickled the Lieutenant's legs
  Until he scarce could stand.

I fear Lieutenant's nap was sham —
  Was merely a disguise —
To fathom really how far boys
  A Frog did idolize!
Quite satisfied with this attempt,
  Lieutenant rubbed his knee,
Pretending, to these tormentors,
  He thought it was a flea.
With courteous smile and merry wink,
  He then said he was ready; .
And Herbert braced himself the while
  To hold Lieutenant steady.

CROCIO FROG'S SONG.

Calmly by the brookside,
  Glad to be alone,
Professor Frog was sitting,
  Trying his bass tone.

Boy, with red lips parted
  By mischievous smile,
Flings a clod at Professor,
  Stops his notes awhile.

Smothered little snicker,
  I much grieve to say,
Came from every child
  On that July day.

Professor reappearing
  In among the reeds,
Wishes boys were up to
  Fewer of such deeds.

Boy again now spies him,
  And another aim
Causes poor Professor
  To feel rather lame.

Grey and Herbert groan
  In loud concert dread;
Wildly call for ashes
  To put upon their heads.

Arthur, too, succumbs,
  Slips down in a mass;
Stops up both his ears
  With green wads of grass.

" Losing time for practice,
   Sore along my thigh,
On some other Leader
   Frogs must to-night rely."

Nearly broken-hearted
   At this state of things,
Professor warmly wishes
   He could borrow wings.

Herbert straightway fashions,
   From a pumpkin leaf,
A startling brace of wings
   To give such grief relief.

Birds are not molested,
   Professor here bethinks;
Happy Jays and Robins!
   Happy Bobolinks!

Drowsy grows Professor,
   Drops off in a nap;
A good Fairy fits him
   To a dreaming-cap.

Dreams he's under rushes,
  Croaking strange content;
Leaping by the brookside
  Without chastisement.

Basking in sweet sunshine,
  Trying thorough bass,
Leading of an evening
  In his proper place.

Feels no painful shyness
  Of that species boy!
Hails him as a comrade,
  With a smile of joy!

Professor slowly wakes up,
  Sees the situation!
But his brief dream gives him
  Feelings of elation.

Immediately he limps off
  To "Frogs' Music Hall;"
Breathlessly arrives there —
  Stands before them all.

Hurriedly proposes
  A speech in place of song,
For he has some wondrous
  News to give that throng!

With consent unanimous
  He at once begins;
Tells them "soon the boys
  Will repent them of their sins —

"Not one single clod
  At a Frog be thrown,
And a boy be scarcely
  From an angel known!"

Drawing rather heavily
  On imagination,
Old Professor threw those Frogs
  In mighty agitation!

Caucuses were called,
  And Delegates appointed
To wait upon the boys —
  Confirm this news disjointed!

Those Delegates! O never
  Did one of them come back!
Perhaps a few wet clods
  Did drop upon their track!

Lieutenant Frog, in venturing
  This gentle supposition,
Looked firmly at the sky
  In awful superstition.

Possessing so much suavity,
  How could he comprehend
That aught save clouds discourteous
  Those fateful clods could send?

Eighteen young eyes did gravely
Investigate the sky;
But not a voice was raised
This charge to falsify.

Lieutenant Frog then hasted
To finish up his song,
And tender quite a good gift
Which he had brought along.

Lieutenant winked and blushed —
　"Meant not to intrude;
But would the present company
　Summon fortitude

"To appropriate a gift,—
　A wondrous Thinking Cap,—
Sprung one hundred years ago
　From old Professor's nap?"

Having ended speech and song,
　Lieutenant Frog withdrew,
And the most tremendous cheers
　His hind legs did pursue.

MR. AND MRS. WOODPECKER.

MR. WOODPECKER
was early abroad,
Tapping old trees with his
strong little bill;
Mrs. Woodpecker, with anx-
ious concern,
Watched with bright eyes for
Woodpecker's return.

Never before had he tarried
so long;
Simple their marketing—
that she well knew.
Ruffled, disturbed, by this
queer state of things,
Mrs. Woodpecker arose on
her wings.

27

Their favorite pear-tree was white with sweet
    blooms;
Mrs. W. detected the fragrance afar.
Right in the teeth of a scent-ladened breeze
She flew to this tree, feeling quite ill at ease.

Mr. Woodpecker, on a blossoming twig,
Was revolving a subject disturbing his mind;
A smart little peck on the back of his neck
Sufficed to give his meditations a check.

Aroused, Mr. Woodpecker flirted his wings,
And briefly explained to his brisk little wife
"That, but for the presence of a party unknown,
He should with the breakfast have back again
    flown.

"The speed which he daily was accustomed to use
In tapping this tree, he was forced to suspend;
The party so narrowly watching them now
Had been swinging an hour upon that low bough."

Mrs. Woodpecker offered her fair self as sentinel,
If Mr. Woodpecker would then tap the tree;

But it was not in wise Mr. Woodpecker's creed
With the day's marketing then to proceed.

"How long is the party unknown going to stay?"
Mrs. Woodpecker asked, with a swift sidelong
    glance.
"Uncertain. I fear he has no business habits.
He may be the party who snared the young
    rabbits."

"Oh, indeed!" with an uncomplimentary toss;
"The eggs will be chilled, if I do not return."
Back to the hollow, wherein was their nest,
Mrs. Woodpecker flew, with fear swelling her
    breast.

On Woodpecker's return, his dear wife was in
    tears;
Refusing to eat, quite dejectedly low.
Woodpecker then solemnly stood on one foot,
Her case he reviewed and in many ways put.

He felt for that day life to him was a riddle —
Conundrum which he had no power to solve.
    3 *

"Heigh-ho!" Mr. Woodpecker at length said aloud;
"My spirits will rise, although troubles crowd.

"This sweet morning air is so good for one's
    throat,
And such a fine, friendly warmth in the sun's
    manner;
To Madame my wife, who is in a sad dream,
I fear quite a heartless young fellow I seem."

Woodpecker's soliloquy came to an end;
Harsh and discordant sounds smote on their ears:
Mrs. Woodpecker, in a flutter and tremble,
Could now no longer her dark fears dissemble.

"Mr. Woodpecker, won't you just give a look?
Something quite dreadful is going to happen!
In a much better neighborhood lived we last
    year;
How can we in this one our sweet birdies rear?"

"The party unknown again, dear little wife,
With the two who have lingered about here for
    days."

"Well! what are they up to?" Mrs. Woodpecker
    said,
While her poor mother heart grew as heavy as
    lead.

"Brewing a quarrel by the edge of the brook."
"What about, Mr. Woodpecker? can't you deter-
    mine?"
"They push so and crowd that I hardly know
    yet —
The hat of the party unknown is quite wet."

Mrs. Woodpecker took a slight peep now herself,
And uttered a low cry of great consternation.
"Mischief is meant! I see sticks and strings!
Whenever together I see those two things,

"I am morally certain some mischief is up!"
"Dear, we will keep out of it," Woodpecker said;
But Mrs. Woodpecker hopped back to her eggs,
Tasting a cup of woe down to its dregs.

Full well she remembered one direful hour,
When Mr. Grey Rabbit a promenade took,

And on his return he found sticks and strings,
But, alas! not his wife or her babies, poor things!

"Pray, don't borrow trouble," Woodpecker advised,
Regretfully noting her disconsolate air;
But Mrs. Woodpecker replied in a tone
Which sounded like nothing else but a deep
    groan.

Mighty the turbulence grew down below.
"A bit, if you please," Mrs. Woodpecker moaned,
"Of very soft down to stop up my poor ears —"
But just here Woodpecker gave two hearty cheers.

"The party unknown is the best of the lot,"
He said, as he plucked from his breast some soft
    down.
Mrs. Woodpecker's eyes opened quick as a snap,
Refusing the down, "I am glad to hear that."

She flew up quite briskly, gave a sharp little
    glance:
"Ho! ho! he has smashed all the sticks and
    the strings!

THREE TIMES AND A TIGER!

He is not a bad boy, one can plainly perceive;
How came he with bad boys I can hardly
    conceive."

"That sometimes does happen," Woodpecker ob-
    served
With a grave air; "but the party unknown
Is making off now quite away from this set,
And really may be in time for his school yet."

"I think he deserves some sort of salute;
Let us cheer him, Woodpecker—three times and
    a tiger."

C

The Woodpeckers cheered with might and with
    main,
Until Mrs. W. exhausted became,
And once more resettled herself on her nest,
With peace in her household and calm in her
    breast.

OTHER STORIES IN VERSE.

35

MARGIE AND HER FLOWERS.

MARGIE'S FLOWERS.

⟶∘⟨∘⟩∘⟵

WINSOME maiden Margie;
   Bluebells sway beside her,
Chiming to the Fairies,
"Change her to a flower
Through your magic power."

Fairies smile and listen;
   Red Rose whispers shyly,
With enchanting blushes,
And most graceful posé,
"Change her to a Rose."

Slender Sweet-pea climbing
   Up a trellis gayly,
Twines a tender tendril

With bewitching ease —
" May *we* have her, please? "

Mignonnette low spreading —
   Sweet her wandering breath —
Asks with mock demureness —
Coaxing, dear coquette —
" Make her Mignonnette."

Moss Rose faintly flushing
   In her odorous nest,
Captivates a Fairy;
Entreats with charming mien,
" Let her be our Queen."

Violets close gathered
   In shy, purple state,
Waft in sweet, rare incense —
Supplicating prayer —
" Give her to our care."

Lilies in rich chorus,
   Standing tall and fair,
Shining in white splendor,
Sing, " This little girl
Is a priceless Pearl."

COUSINS.

GRACE.

FRAGILE little fairy,
  White as winter's snow,
Graceful and so "airy,"
  Born three years ago.

TOMMY.

Sturdy little Scotchman,
  Hardy, stout, and square,
Thinks that he is really
  Quite a big affair.

GRACE.

Petted, pretty flower,
  Laughing out in glee,
Soon a pearly shower
  From her eyes you see.

39

COUSINS.

TOMMY.

Coolest little fellow,
  Dares you with a wink;
Cares so very slightly
  For aught thât you may think.

GRACE.

Trudging with unsteady feet
  Down the narrow lane;
Ready every one to greet,
  And a smile obtain.

TOMMY.

Looking toward the horses,
  Will not take your hand;
Takes his time, and never minds
  Any reprimand.

GRACE.

Nestles to your loving arms,
  Smiles up in your face;
Wondrous rich in baby charms
  Is this tender Grace.

TOMMY.

Looks with loftiest disdain
  At one's gentle wiles;
Quite a waste, as you will find,
  Of the sweetest smiles.

GRACE.

Stretches up her dimpled hands
  To caress your cheeks,
Pleading with blue, gentle eyes
  For the love she seeks.

TOMMY.

Stretches out a little fist
  In a mimic fight,
Leaving loving adversary
  In a doubtful plight.

4 *

A SECRET.

ONLY the golden sun,
  Rich tropical roses ablow,
Flame-throated birds and silvery waves,
  A charming secret know.

They whispered it close in my ear;
  I promised not to tell!
The secret is safe as a stone
  Dropped deep down in a well.

You would love her sweet blue eyes,
  The sheen of her soft brown hair;
And an innocent way she has,
  None but angels can compare.

The birds, the waves, and the roses,
  The sun up in the sky,
Love dearly this lovely Eunice:
  So why not you and I?

OUR "BABY GREY."

OUR Baby Grey is a wonderful child,
So brown and fat, so wise and wild;
Oh, how can I tell you half that he is —
Of the beauty and grace of his dear little phiz?
He is grave as a judge, and a naughty sprite,
Not a doubtful blessing, but one outright.
He can twist us all with a look of his eye;
Can make us do everything but sigh.
Propound a query, which to know
Straight to the angels one must go.
Ah, Baby Grey! in the future years,
In times of calm or times of tears,
Keep pure thy heart's unstained snow;
Hold fast thy childhood's trust, and know
That talents two, or five, or ten,
Must soon be rendered up again
Into the Lord's deep treasury,
Receiving His own with usury.

43

GONE.

L ITTLE Mamie, fresh and fair,
  Laughing eyes and curly hair,
How I loved you, darling, sweet,
And the patter of your feet
Through the entry up the stairs,
Bringing smiles, beguiling cares.

Ever ready for some play,
From the dawn till close of day;
Lovely, beaming, childish face
Shining with a nameless grace.

Little Mamie, cold and pale,
Shadowed with the mystic veil;
On her brow and lip and hand
The signet of the Better Land.
Who would wake the pulse's beat —
Call the life to those still feet?
Know ye not those curls at rest
Are pillowed on an angel's breast?
That the still and marble face
Is shining with a fadeless grace?

So we reason; thus we speak;
But we cannot dry our cheek.
We shall miss her till the day
God doth wipe all tears away.

www.ingramcontent.com/pod-product-compliance
Lightning Source LLC
Chambersburg PA
CBHW021235260626
47172CB00002B/777